Bear & Katie
in
A Day with Friends

By Loni R. Burchett

Illustrated by Patricia Sweet-MacDonald

To Riley -
Enjoy!
Loni R. Burchett

Other books by Loni Burchett

Bear and Katie in The Great Searsport Caper

Bear and Katie in A Day at Nestlenook Farm

Released 2004

Written by Loni R. Burchett
Illustrated by Patricia Sweet-MacDonald
Edited by Nancy Grossman and Joanie Bennett

Published by
Black Lab Publishing, LLC
P.O. Box 64
Alton, NH 03809
blacklabpub@hotmail.com
www.bearandkatie.com

Printed by Morgan Press, Manchester, NH
603-624-6880
Published and manufactured in the U.S.A.

First Printing: July, 2005

ISBN: 0-9742815-2-2

Dedicated to

Christopher D. Burchett: The most wonderful son and friend.

Bear and Katie forever: Who truly lived up to the old saying, "A dog is a man's best friend."

Special Thanks to the following people:

David Edwards, advisor and life long friend.

Richard Haynes, free lance photographer, artist
and friend. For all the countless hours he spent
helping me to achieve my goals.

Nancy Grossman, artist, writer, editor and
wonderful friend. For her inspiration and
encouragement.

Richard Price, for giving me the information
I needed to write this book.

Pauline Burchett, for her hours of research and advice.

Acknowledgements:

The Price Maple Farm
Route 140
Gilmanton, N.H.

Preface

Maple syrup production in 2004 totaled 934,000 gallons. Vermont it still the largest producing state in New England and the nation with 54 percent of the regions syrup production. Taps in New England make up 58 percent of the nation's maple syrup.

New England taps last year were 4.0 million. Other states with large maple productions, are New Hampshire, Maine, New York, Massachusetts, Connecticut, Wisconsin, Michigan and Ohio. The United States, along with Canada, (our neighbors to the north) supply the world with delicious maple syrup.

NOTE: Bear wears a red collar. Katie prefers to wear a blue scarf.

Bear and Katie always refer to their owners as Dad and Mom.

Table of Contents

Introduction:

New England in the spring is magnificent. It's a lovely time to get out and enjoy the weather. With the snow melting, lakes thawing and the birds and ducks returning to their favorite spots, the sight is beautiful. The New England landscape is dotted with buckets hanging from maple trees. Friendly farmers are anxious to teach visitors all about their sugaring technique, they learned long ago from the Native Americans, who taught their ancestors all about the great sweet taste that came from the maple trees.

Sugaring in New England is a special time of year. In early March to middle April, the maple farmers empty buckets full of sap into a gathering tank. The sap is delivered to a Sugarhouse and there they begin the process of making their syrup. Taking a drive down a country road in New England you may see smoke coming from a sugarhouse or (sugar shack.) It's a special time for New Englanders and for Bear and Katie to visit a maple farm or to join in on a maple festival. Bear and Katie enjoy the hayrides along with getting a lot of pats on the head by passer-bys. Visiting a maple farm is a lot of fun.

Many of the farms invite the public on tours along with giving out a sample of their syrup and candy. Some provide a delicious pancake breakfast. Shops with beautifully wrapped gift packages are also available.

Bear enjoys watching the sugar-man make the syrup, while Katie is anxious to try a sample. "So come along with Bear and Katie to a Maple Farm!"

A Day with Friends

It's springtime in New England and what a beautiful sight. The trees are beginning to bud everywhere. Maple farmers are busy finishing their long chore of gathering up sap from the maple trees. Frozen lakes have melted, birds are chirping and the ducks are returning to their favorite spots. The loons have returned and by summer their chicks will be born and will be riding them "piggyback." Their strange haunting sounds can be heard on lakes all over New England. It's a happy time for two black labs that have been cooped up all winter.

Every morning after breakfast, Dad lets Bear and Katie out onto the porch to enjoy the fresh morning air. Katie always jumps up, puts her paws on the railing and looks off towards the lake with excitement. And Bear always flops down at the top of the stairs, one paw tucked under her chest.

Bear loves to chase squirrels, so Katie plays lookout for Bear. She peers out at the trees around the lake and down along the shore and back to the trees again. She can see a long way from the porch. The porch is one of Bear and Katie's favorite spots.

"I don't see anything yet," says Katie, with a soft whine.

Lifting her head, Bear woofs, "It's still early. You just keep looking."

Bear lays her head back down, but keeps her eyes and ears open. She's ready to take off the minute there's a good enough reason.

Katie continues her patrol, and then looks back to Bear again. "I can't wait to go swimming," Katie grins, looking out at the water.

Bear lifts her head again, just slightly, gives Katie a long look and shakes her head. "Uh oh. Here we go again and it's just barely spring! Katie, you're always getting yourself into trouble, especially when you take off on your own. You know it's much too cold to go swimming in the lake," she sighs. "You'll freeze, you know!"

"You're right!" yelps Katie. "It isn't warm enough yet, -- but a lab can dream."

Katie takes a long look toward the lake and turns to Bear. "You know, warm weather is just around the corner, and I will be out there as soon as Dad says it's okay," she continues.

Bear lifts her head for the third time and looks straight at Katie. "Who do you think you're kidding?" Bear asks sternly. "You go there even when people are at the beach, when you know dogs are not allowed. Mom has to come and get you because you never obey the rules," she grumbles.

Katie lays her head down and rests it on her paws. "Well... you know how I love to swim, and when I hear kids playing, I just can't help myself!"

Katie decides to change the subject and give Bear a little of her own medicine. She turns and stares directly into Bear's eyes.

"By the way, you have a lot of nerve to talk about me. You have to go everywhere in the truck with Dad. If you don't get to go, you pout, get mad and chew up Dad's slippers."

"So, I love going for rides," says Bear, indignant. "So what? I don't want to miss out on anything. Going for rides is ... soothing for me." Bear lets out a little woof that sound like a *harrumph.

Suddenly, Katie jumps to attention, with her tail standing straight and her eyes glued to a tall pine tree across the other side of the yard.

"What's that, Bear? Oh boy! It's a squirrel! And he is heading for that tall pine tree," she says in a soft whisper.

Bear rises to her feet, takes a long look towards the trees and looks back at Katie. "Let's go!" she says.

The two dogs leap off the porch, running as fast as they can, chasing the squirrel across the yard and running so fast that all you can hear are the thumps of paws pounding on the ground.

---

*Harrumph, *The show of clearing one's throat*

Katie reaches the tall pine tree, with Bear right behind her.

The squirrel quickly makes his way up the tree and takes his place on a large limb.

Katie runs around the tree and around it again, sniffing the ground. Bear looks up and down the tree and up again, and then she finally spots the squirrel. Bear begins to bark and then Katie begins to bark, too.

The squirrel, looking down, recognizes her old friends Bear and Katie. "Hey! Hey!" the squirrel shouts, "Bear and Katie, it's me, your old pal, Chestnut!"

Peering up into the tree, Bear and Katie barely see Chestnut, hiding behind a branch on the large tree limb. Bear and Katie greet Chestnut with a friendly whine.

"Where have you been?" Bear calls up to their friend. "We haven't seen you in such a long time."

Chewing on an acorn, Chestnut peeks out from behind the branch to answer her. "Well, I've been on the other side of the lake, actually. I found a really nice tree to make my home for the winter. A really nice condo, know what I mean?" With a flip of his bushy tail, the squirrel continues, "I decided to come over to see how you girls have been doing."

Katie responds with a very soft bark. "I'm glad to see you made it through all those snowstorms. We sure had a lot of them this year."

"Oh, you're right about that! Thanks for being so concerned," Chestnut calls down. "Oh, by the way, can I ask you something?"

he shouts, looking at Katie. "I've always wondered why you and Bear chase us squirrels, but when you catch up to us, you just sit and bark at us. You never try to hurt us," says the curious squirrel, nibbling on the nut in his hand.

Bear laughs. "Oh, we just like to play with you guys, and it helps us burn off the ol' calories."

Looking down, Chestnut knows he can't be caught way up in the tree and decides to tease Bear and Katie. Laughing, he agrees, "You two could stand to lose a few pounds."

Bear lets out a few growls.

Chestnut lets out a little squirrel laugh and then calls down to Bear and Katie, "I've got to go, girls. My friends are waiting for me. We've got to go shopping around for food."

Katie is surprised. "I always thought you squirrels gathered enough food to last into spring," she ruffs.

Chestnut nods. "We usually do, but we thought this was going to be another mild winter like last year. I guess we didn't listen to the groundhog report. Well, we squirrels can make a mistake or two. But we better not make many. I hate hunting for acorns in the snow." He nods again, along with a slight grumble.

Bear and Katie bark in agreement with Chestnut. They say their goodbyes to their friend with a double bark. Chestnut jumps across to another limb and knocks his head on a branch with an "Oops!"

"Maybe I'll catch up with you later today over at Price's Maple Farm. I hear Mr. Price is boiling his last batch of sap," he yells as he shows off, leaping from one branch to another, until he is clear out of sight.

"Mmm, yes. Maple syrup!" barks Bear, joyfully. "Oh, yes, let's do go!"

Bear nudges Katie. "Let's take a walk along the lake and then through the woods. We might run into some more of our friends on our way to the maple farm," she suggests.

"Sounds good to me!" responds Katie, with a pleasant bark.

The two labs stop every few feet to sniff the ground. Bear, who's in the lead, suddenly stops. "Katie, do you smell that?" she snorts, wiggling her nose.

"I sure do! And I don't like that smell at all," cries Katie as she raises her paw to cover her nose.

Bear and Katie begin to back up slowly and carefully turn around, when Katie suddenly shouts, "Watch out, Bear!"

But it's too late. Bear and Katie are face to face with a skunk, and that skunk has his tail raised straight up in the air!

"Hold it there!" whines Bear softly, not to frighten the skunk. Bear is well aware of what happens when a skunk is frightened. She's had her run-ins with skunks.

Katie jumps in. "Well, hi there...uh, Stinky," says Katie. "How was your winter?"

Bear turns to Katie with a stern look. "Be careful what you say, Katie!" she whispers. "We don't want him to spray us."

"Oh, okay, gotcha!" Katie whispers back to Bear. Then, in her friendliest, gentlest, sweetest bark, she says again to the skunk, "Well...hello, there...ol' Stinky, ol' pal!" And she and Bear begin again to step backwards, taking one careful step at a time.

"We're Bear and Katie," ruffs Bear as she backs away. "What's your name?"

"I'm Sneaky the skunk," says the skunk in a most friendly voice. He doesn't budge, and his tail remains quite upright.

"I thought your name might be Stinky," smiles Katie.

"Nope. It's Sneaky. I sneak up on everything!" he snorts, waving his tail just a little bit *menacingly.

"Well, we sure are glad to meet you," says Bear, nudging Katie to agree with her.

"Oh, oh, yes! It's sure nice to meet you," Katie tells Sneaky, with her paw still covering her nose.

The skunk seems friendly enough, the two labs are thinking, as he lowers his tail just a bit. Bear stops backing away and grins a big smile at the little skunk. Sneaky looks surprised.

"I wish the other animals in the woods wouldn't run from me. I don't have many friends, you know," he tells Bear and Katie, hanging his head.

*Menacingly, *A threatening manner*

"But you really are very good looking," says Bear, kindly. "I really like that white stripe down your back."

"Why, thank you," Sneaky responds. "It's kind of my trade mark. You know what I mean?" The plump little skunk wobbles around and around in a crooked little circle, showing off his long white stripe so his new friends can get a good look at him. By the time he finishes his second circle, his tail is dragging on the ground.

"Well, now that we know you won't spray us, we would love to spend some time with you," chuckles Katie.

"That's great!" snorts the once unhappy skunk. "Now I have some friends."

"That's right," smiles Bear. "In fact, we are

on our way to Mr. Price's Maple Farm. Would you like to tag along?"

"Thanks you for asking, girls, but I have too many things to do today, hunting and all, you know," says Sneaky.

"But you're going to be missing out on a taste of Mr. Price's delicious maple syrup," barks Bear.

"Well...I don't think the way I smell would mix too well with that great smell of maple boiling," cries the cute little skunk. You know, I do have a funny odor .

"Oh! We never even noticed," answers Katie turning her head and twitching her nose.

"You didn't?" says Sneaky. "Well...maybe the next time you go I will tag along with you.

But I really have some things I want to do," he tells them with a happy wave of his tail and a fat little wobble.

"Well then, we'll meet up with you again soon," ruffs Bear. "Then we'll have more time to visit."

"I'll see you then," replies the skunk, as he wobbles away, flopping his tail from side to side.

Moving on, Bear looks straight ahead, her eyes searching the ground for something to hunt. Suddenly she halts, quickly turns to Katie, and then quietly ruffs, "Katie! Do you see what I see?"

Katie's ears perk up. "I do indeed. It's a man putting bird food in a feeder box. It's much too early to be putting bird food in a

feeder box! Everyone knows that in early spring the black bears wander in people's yards searching for food after a long winter's nap. They always go to the feeder boxes. That man is going to be in danger if he doesn't watch out!" she whines.

Katie stands stock-still. "I sure don't want to run into a bear," answers Katie in her tiniest dog whisper.

Bear steps carefully aside, barking with agreement. She shakes her head with dismay. "I have to do something!" she says.

Bear barks, yips and howls, trying to warn the man away. All the uproar distracts the man, who stops what he is doing to see what the *hullabaloo is about. The man begins to follow the barks, yips and howls. Bear and

---

*Hullabaloo, *Up-roar*

Katie lead him on a merry chase, doubling
back to where the bag of birdseed sits by the
feeder. Bear grabs it with her teeth, runs off to
the woods with it and drags it far out into a
stream near by.

The man spots Bear with his bag of birdseed
in her mouth. "Hey! Come back here! That's
my bird food that you've got!" shouts the
angry man.

But Bear ignores the man, who is quickly
catching up to her. "I said come back here!"

The man realizes he is getting nowhere with
an angry voice. He decides to use a different
approach. "Here doggie, doggie," cries the
man. "You sure are a pretty lab. Can you give
me that bag of bird food please?" he asks, with
his hand reaching out to Bear and a snarl on
his face.

But Bear is too smart for the man. She knows when someone is trying to trick her. She continues out into the stream.

Katie lets out a loud bark to warn Bear. "Drop the bag and get out of the water fast and follow me!" She yells to Bear with another strong bark.

Bear does as Katie tells her and drops the bag of bird food and watches it float down stream.

"He won't be feeding any more bears today!" woofs Katie with a big dog grin on her face.

Bear wades out of the water and shakes herself off. "Darned tootin' he won't! And we may have saved his life," she says.

"Well, I sure hope he doesn't do that again," ruffs Katie as she turns to look out towards the stream.

Off Bear trots, especially pleased with herself.

The man just stands there, watching his bag of bird food float away. "I wonder what got into those dogs?" he thinks to himself, shaking his head as he turns to walk away.

The two labs continue on their journey. It's a beautiful day, for the beginning of spring. Bear and Katie are going to take in as much of it as they can.

Suddenly, Bear lets out a short bark. "Katie! Over here! I think I found something!"

Katie bounds over to Bear and pushes past her to get a good look at a hole in the ground that Bear has come across, shoving her nose right in.

And for all her trouble, Katie gets a pop on the nose. She steps back, surprised, shaking her head.

"You just had to stick your nose in there, didn't you, Katie?" Bear chuckles out a bark with a wiggle of her tail. Katie, a bit embarrassed, ignores Bear. "Why, it's a groundhog hole!" says Katie.

Without warning, a groundhog pops up, rubbing his eyes, looking very *perturbed by the intruders. "Go away!" he shouts angrily. "I already did my job this year. I came out. I saw my shadow. I told the world that there would be six more weeks of wintry weather. So you can just go away!"

Katie is impressed. "You mean... you're that groundhog!"

"Yes, I'm that groundhog. Well...actually, I'm Grady G. the Groundhog, Punxsutawney Phil's New England cousin, for your

---

*Perturbed, *Irritable, cross*

information!   And I'd be much obliged if you two black labs would just clear out and let a *hibernator get the rest of his sleep."

---

*Hibernator, *To hide away for a long time; To pass the winter*

"But...Grady G. it's been more than six weeks," woofs Bear. "It's the first week of April."

"I know, I know," snorts the very perturbed groundhog. "But this year was a bit colder than usual. That happens sometimes."

"Oh my!" ruffs Katie with a sneaky grin. "We woke you up, didn't we? But since you're awake now anyway...how about answering a question?" she continues. "What's it actually like, advising the world every year on if we are going to have six more weeks of winter?"

The groundhog answers with a sigh, "Well, between you and me, it wouldn't be that bad, if they'd just keep all those cameras away. I hate cameras flashing in my eyes. I see spots for hours afterwards." He shuts his eyes at the memory. "Spots make it hard to get back to sleep," he adds, with a yawn.

Katie thinks about it for a moment. "But look at all the publicity you get!" she barks.

The groundhog shakes his head and snorts. "Who wants publicity?" he asks Katie.

"Well, I would, for one," Bear jumps in, thinking about all the cameras and lights. "I wish someone was out there waiting to take a picture of us, two beautiful, lovely, precious, sweet, gentle..."

Katie interrupts. "Okay, okay, Bear! Enough about how gorgeous you are. You're always bragging about yourself, Miss Prissy!"

Changing the subject, Grady G. chuckles at Bear and Katie, then he begins to count on his fingers. "Let me see...best I can figure, I can sneak in one more week of rest. Any chance you two would go on your way so I can get the rest of my rest?"

"One more week! "I think you are just a lazy groundhog," Bear tells him.

"Well... they don't call me a ground...hog for nothing," he yawns. "I just happen to enjoy sleeping a little longer than some of the others."
"We thought you might like to go with us to Price's Maple Farm," suggests Katie.

"No, no!" grumbles Grady G. "I need to get some more sleep."

"Well then," whispers Bear, "see you another time when you've finished your nap."

The groundhog yawns. "Oh, yes! Thanks for the warning. Then I'll have to put up with you two chasing me all summer long."

"It's all in a day's fun," Katie smiles. "We'll be going now."

As Bear and Katie leave their friend, the last thing they hear from the groundhog as he disappears back into his little hole in the ground is, "See you around Bear and Katie...and watch out for grumpy groundhogs. You could get punched in the nose, you know," he laughs with an echo from under the ground.

Boiling the Sap!

Bear and Katie turn to head straight for
Price's Maple Farm. As they approach the farm,
they hear a slight noise behind a tree. It's their
friend Duchess, a beautiful deer.

"Hello Duchess! How are you today?" barks Bear, as she rubs up against a sign that reads, "Welcome to Price's Maple Farm."

"I'm fine, thank you," Duchess snorts. I'm on my way to the maple farm."

"So are we!" bark Bear and Katie together.

"I can smell the wonderful aroma of maple boiling," Duchess continues. "I love it when Mr. Price gives us a taste of his fine maple syrup. I have a real sweet tooth for maple," she adds with a smile.

Bear, Katie, and Duchess walk on towards the entrance of the maple farm and who do they find there already climbing down the tree? Why, it's Chestnut!

Mr. Price opens the door. "Well! What a

wonderful surprise!" he exclaims. "It's Bear and Katie, Chestnut and... Duchess! Well, come in, come in," he laughs.

"We've come to learn all about how you make maple syrup," barks Katie.

"Well, you're just in time," says Mr. Price. "First I have to collect all the sap from the trees, so follow me, my little friends."

Bear, Katie, Chestnut and Duchess follow Mr. Price outside to where the buckets are hanging on the trees.

"Before we gather all the sap and boil it, I will tell you a story that I tell every year to my children," says Mr. Price.

Bear, Katie, Duchess and Chestnut are excited to hear Mr. Price's story. Bear and Katie sit down, while Duchess leans on a tree and Chestnut climbs onto a small limb.

"It happened a long time ago," he begins.

"You see, there was a maple farmer who lived right up there." He points to a huge hill. "It's called Taylor Notch, named for old Billy Taylor. But folks around here called him Willy. Every year at the big maple festival in town, Willy would bring syrup, candy and the finest maple fudge you ever ate. He was known for making the most maple syrup in all of New England. Old Willy would brag about having more buckets on his trees than anyone else in New Hampshire and Vermont." He continues with a short pause. "But, of course, he really didn't know, seeing he never got too far from Taylor Notch.

"One early spring, we had a sudden storm. It must have snowed two feet that year. It was during the time of the festival. Well, old Willy never showed up with his syrup, candy and fudge. Town folks got worried. They knew that Willy loved to bring his famous maple fudge and his syrup to the festival for everyone to enjoy. The town residents got together a search party. Why, we searched for days. One man found tracks up there on the notch that seemed to keep circling around and around some of the maple trees. But old Willy was never found. No...he was never found!"

Mr. Price takes a deep breath, looks at all of his animal friends and continues. "They say that every year, in the early spring, people see those very tracks in the snow. It must be the ghost of Willy trying to find his way back to his sugar house." Mr. Price looks up toward the hills they all know as Taylor Notch. Then he looks back at Bear and Katie, Duchess and Chestnut.

Bear and Katie look at each other and just shiver. Duchess takes a deep breath and sighs. Chestnut drops an acorn on the ground. "That is scary!" says Chestnut. "You can bet I won't be climbing any of those trees," he tells them.

Mr. Price just smiles. "Well, now that I have told my story, let's gather up some sap."

Bear and Katie try not to think about the story of old Willy Taylor. Bear doesn't want to

appear scared and neither does Katie or
Duchess.

They all begin to help Mr. Price with his
chore. Bear and Katie are busy carrying the
empty buckets back to the trees, gripping them
with their teeth. Duchess walks around and
let's them know when the gathering tank is
full. Chestnut sits in the tree and watches
from above.

"Where does the sap come from?" asks Bear, as she watches it drip into one of the buckets.

"Well, it takes good cold nights and then a nice warm morning for the sap to travel up from the roots to the trunk of the trees and on up into the limbs," he tells them. "I drill a two-inch hole and put a spout into it for the sap to drain into the buckets. Each bucket holds about 16 quarts of sap. It's emptied into this large tub and then taken to the sugar house, where we begin to boil the sap."

"How many gallons of sap do you gather each day?" asks Chestnut, nibbling on another acorn.

Mr. Price rubs his chin as he considers Chestnut's question. "About 450 to 600 gallons, I do believe. I have to empty the buckets every day. A farmer has to have a lot of buckets," he tells Chestnut with a wink.

"Wow! That must make a lot of syrup!" barks Bear.

"Well, it takes about 35 gallons of sap to make 1 gallon of syrup. On a really good day, I can make 20 gallons of syrup. Now it's time to deliver all this sap to the sugar house," says Mr. Price.

Once at the sugarhouse, they all find a comfortable spot. Bear and Katie sit as close as they can to watch how the steaming sap boils into delicious maple syrup. Duchess watches from the open door, while Chestnut enjoys watching from the floor, nibbling on his favorite meal, another acorn.

"First, I empty the sap into the holding tank. From there it travels to the pre-heater," says Mr. Price.

"Once the sap goes to the rear boiling pan, it travels to the front finishing pan of the evaporator. This is when the syrup is finished. The hotter the fire, the faster it boils."

"At what temperature does it become syrup?" asks Duchess.

"At 219 degrees it becomes syrup. Then, you can smell the sweet smell of maple," he tells Duchess with a big smile. Mr. Price knows that Duchess loves the taste of fine maple syrup.

"What is the difference between light syrup and dark syrup?" Katie asks with her usual curious expression.

"Keeping equipment clean, gathering sap daily and boiling down the sap to syrup as soon as possible makes for lighter syrup," Mr.

Price tells her. "Once the trees begin to bud, it starts getting darker."

"I enjoy making the syrup the old -fashioned way," Mr. Price continues. "I still use a wood-burning stove. I gather firewood all summer long, until I have enough to last through the boiling season."

"When is it ready to put in cans or bottles?" asks Bear.

"First, the syrup is drawn from the boiling pan. Then, it is strained through wool cloth, sometimes called wool hats or finishing strainers. We use a pre-strainer inside of the wool hat. It's like an extra large coffee filter. It strains the syrup before it goes through the finishing strainer, the wool hat. The pre-strainers are changed regularly so I don't have to wash the wool strainer as often. Then the syrup is canned or bottled at 185 degrees. It is sealed in the containers, so they won't need refrigeration until they're opened. Then it goes to the stores."

Mr. Price has a ladle in his hand. "Now! All of you gather around and get a taste of Mr. Price's finest maple syrup!"

They all push their way closer to Mr. Price, who holds the ladle out. He gives each of his animal friends just a tiny taste of the sweet maple syrup.

Then he says good-bye to them. Bear, Katie and Duchess leave with a smile, while Chestnut leaps up a tree and disappears into the branches.

Bear and Katie bark, "Thank you and good-bye," to Mr. Price as they go. He knows that next year they will be back again.

"I think it's time we head for home," says Bear.

"Do you care if I walk with you for a bit?" snorts Duchess.

"We would love the company," answers Katie.

The three of them pass by the entrance to Mr. Price's farm and head back through the woods until they finally reach the lake.

Duchess stops. "Listen to that!" she warns Bear and Katie. "That loud hooting sound is a loon," she continues. "They make that sound and flap their wings and do a crazy dance on the water when they think they are being threatened. But I find it quite entertaining," she says with a quiet snort.

"Let's go talk to the loon," says Katie, very curious. "I would love to meet a loon," cries Bear, all excited.

The three of them arrive at the lake.

"Well, no wonder the loon is hooting. There's a raccoon at the edge of the lake," woofs Bear.

"That's Reggie the raccoon," snorts Duchess. "He's very nice and lots of fun."

"Hello, Reggie," snorts Duchess. Reggie greets Duchess with a smile, as he rubs his paws across his eyes. "Well, hello, Duchess, nice to see you.

"These are my friends Bear and Katie," Duchess tells Reggie.

"I like those rings around your eyes and your tail," ruffs Katie.

"Well...Thank you for noticing! Everyone I meet says I'm pretty. It must be so," he says as he turns around and around showing off his pretty eyes and tail.

"What are you doing here,?" snorts Duchess.

"I was washing some acorns when this crazy loon pops up out of the water and flaps his wings at me, scaring me half to death!" he chirps.

The loon begins to hoot, flap it's wings and do its dance. "Go away! You're a little too close for comfort," cries the loon.

"We are Bear and Katie, this is our friend, Duchess, and this is Reggie the raccoon," says Katie. "We are very friendly, Mr. Loon."

"Well, then, what do you want?" he hoots.

"Can you make that haunting sound for us?" asks Katie politely.

"You are so beautiful." Bear tells the loon. "I love your pretty feathers. They look almost like a checker-board. And your amazing red eyes are so interesting."

The loon sits up and points his beak in the air.

"Well thank you! I love a good compliment," says the loon.

"Where do you go during the winter?" Asks Duchess with her pretty deer face.

"We go down toward the Gulf coast. You know, down around Florida and that part of the country. Then we return in the spring," he tells them. "Some of us come back here. And some of us even go as far as Wisconsin, and even into Canada. I'll tell you, it's really hard to find a good lake these days. So many people leave fishing line with hooks in the waters. It makes it dangerous for us," the Loon confides, with a hoot.

"I know what you mean," snorts Duchess. "It's a dangerous life for us deer, too, especially during the fall of the year. Hunters, you know," she tells the loon, shaking her head.

Katie jumps in. "Why do loons carry their

little chicks on their backs? I didn't know a
duck could do that."

"Okay, first of all, I am not a duck. I am a
bird! We loons are birds that live on the water.

And second, we are the only birds that carry our chicks piggyback," he continues. "We do it to protect them. We like to keep our chicks close to us."

"How far can you dive?" asks Bear.

"We can dive 200 feet! And we can stay under water for five minutes or more," he answers, with a loud wailing sound that is, in fact, a bit haunting.

"Boy! That sound gives me the willies," says Katie with a soft bark.

"Willies, did you say?" snorts Duchess, giving Bear and Katie a chilling look. The three of them think about the story Mr. Price told them about old Willy Tucker.

"I...I better re-phrase that. I mean that

sound is a bit haunting. No, no, I...mean that sound is a bit strange. Yes! Strange. That's what I mean," mumbles Katie.

The loon takes a dive and pops back up from the water. "I have to go hunt for fish, and Mrs. Loon is waiting for me. It was fun meeting you, Bear, Katie and Duchess.

"We are glad we met you, too, Mr. Loon," ruffs Bear. "I hope we see you again, because I would love to see you with a chick riding on your back." Just remind me if you see me again. Otherwise, I'll just hoot, flap my wings and do my little dance on the water," he tells them.

And... I would love to take a swim with you sometime," says Katie. "I'm an excellent swimmer, but not much of a diver." She laughs out a bark, as they turn to walk away.

"And I can also swim," snorts Duchess.

Bear, Katie, and Duchess begin to walk toward home. "Well, I guess it's time for me to return to the woods," says Duchess. "I'll see you two somewhere down the road."

"You can be sure of that!" says Bear. "Be sure to stay away from Taylor Notch," warns Katie.

Bear and Katie say good-bye to their friends Duchess and Reggie the Raccoon. They spot Chestnut jumping through the trees with an acorn in his mouth. They wonder if Grady G. really went back to sleep, and if Sneaky the skunk will find more friends. They talk about how much they learned about the making of maple syrup. They know they will never forget the ghost story Mr. Price told them! That scared them half out of their wits. And of course they will be watching and listening for Mr. Loon.

The two labs spot Dad standing on the porch. They know he will be waiting with treats. "Time for a treat! Oh boy, oh boy, oh boy!" woofs Bear. "Maybe we'll get a chewy and a biscuit. We better get going!" shouts Katie. "I'll beat you to the house!"

Bear may want to get her treat, but she's not a lab to rush. "Be my guest. I prefer taking life a little bit slow. Take time to smell the roses ... or the maple syrup, like today!" She ruffs.

Katie slows up and waits for her friend Bear. The two labs head for the house, eager to enjoy their treats and take a nice, long nap.

"This sure was a fun day with friends," barks Bear. "It was a great day with friends," agrees Katie.

The End

In Memory Of Bear and Katie

*Although "A Day with Friends" is Volume 3 of the
Bear and Katie Series, it was the first story I wrote
about Bear and Katie.*

*Bear loved to be photographed and to show off her
tricks. She loved to retrieve a ball. Bear loved to
wade in the water and dunk her head but would not
swim. She was always protective of her family and of
Katie. She was very smart and we always said, "If
dogs could learn to talk, Bear would be one of them."
She loved attention from everyone and enjoyed hugs
from children. Bear was prim and proper. She would
walk around a mud puddle to keep from getting dirty.
She was a good friend and companion. Bear was
always ready to go for a ride. After I wrote dozens of
Bear and Katie stories she became sick with cancer.
We lost our beautiful Bear on November 11, 2003
just before the Searsport Caper Vol. 1, went into print.
So... we took Bears picture and had it silhouetted.
She is the logo for Black Lab Publishing LLC.*

Katie was just the opposite from Bear. She didn't care about showing off tricks; just show her where the water is! Katie would swim as long as someone would throw something into the water for her. She had a mind of her own and was forever... running off to the lake. Katie could be found anywhere you could hear children playing. Although Bear would walk around a mud puddle, Katie would walk right through it. She loved her best friend Bear. Katie was a bit reckless and mischievous but lots of fun. She loved to have her tummy rubbed and enjoyed hugs by anyone. Katie was friendly and truly...a lovable black lab. She loved to play Frisbee and to go on walks. Katie was diagnosed with cancer in February. We lost our precious Katie on June 7, 2005. "She was the sweetest dog that ever lived."

Bear and Katie left lots of memories that will live on through their stories. I am happy to share these two fun-loving dogs with everyone.

Loni R. Burchett
Author

About Bear

Bear is gentle, caring, very intelligent and quick thinking. She always obeys the rules and loves playing the role of Katie's protector. Her hobbies include riding around with Dad, retrieving balls and chasing squirrels. Bear welcomes a pat on the head from everyone she meets. Bear, a female black lab/shepherd mix, wandered her way to our doorstep when she was only six weeks old. Bear always wears a collar.

About Katie

Katie is fun loving, a bit too friendly, and is always getting into trouble. She loves her best friend Bear and knows Bear will always come to her rescue. Katie finds trouble everywhere she goes. Her hobbies are swimming, retrieving balls and frisbee. She was rescued at the last minute from a dog pound when she was six months old. Katie is a female black lab. Katie prefers to wear a scarf.

About the Author

Loni R. Burchette was born in Ashland, Kentucky. It was only when she moved to New Hampshire that she finally found a place she could love as much as the beautiful "Blue Grass State" she hails from. Along with her husband and four of her five children, she now makes the Lakes Region of New Hampshire her home. Her hobbies are writing, art and traveling.

About the Illustrator

Patricia Sweet-MacDonald was born in Clearwater, Florida. She moved to New Hampshire in 2002, with her husband, Michael and two children, Alison and Brendan. She started painting at age 5 and has never quit.

Future Bear and Katie Books

A Riverboat Ride on the Ohio

A Day at the Beach and Katie Gets Arrested

Bear and Katie at the Kentucky Derby
   "Run for the Roses"

Lost in the White Mountains

Bear and Katie See the Big Apple

In the Badlands with Mr. Wanbli (Eagle)

A Day with Mato the Bear

Visit our website at www.bearandkatie.com

Be sure to visit a Maple Farm when traveling through the northeast. Here are some that you might enjoy. Learn about Maple sugaring, enjoy the candy and syrup while browsing through the gift shops.

Ranson Farms
Mountain Road
Riverton, CT

Maple Grove Farms
Portland Street
St. Johnsbury, VT

Williams Farms
Rt. 30
Cornwall, VT

Strawberry Hill Farms
Back Road
Skowheagan, ME

Harvest Hill Farms
Bakertown Road
West Poland, ME

Bo's Sugar Shack
Steefer Farm Road
Sugar Hill, N.H.

Price Maple Farm
Rt. 140
Gilmanton, NH

Brookledge Sugarhouse
Haydenville Road
Wheatly, MA

North Hadley Sugarshack
River Drive
Hadley, MA

Patterson Farms
Gurney Road
Sabinsville, PA

Wright Farms, Inc.
Laidlow Road
Franklinville, NY

In Canada
Maple Orchard Farms of Canada
14 Gray Road
Bracebridge, Ontario, Canada